繪本童話中國
A Chinese Folktale

老鼠娶新娘
THE MOUSE BRIDE

作者 ● 張玲玲　　繪者 ● 劉宗慧

遠流出版公司
YUAN-LIOU PUBLISHING CO.,LTD.

A long time ago, in a large farmhouse in Taiwan, there was a mouse village built in the corner of a stone wall.

The head mouse of this small community had been thinking of his daughter's marriage. She was young and pretty, and had attracted many young fellows. But her father just could not decide which of the many suitors should be his son-in-law. He thought about this day and night, and finally made up his mind -- he would set up a fair test, and let the test itself choose the best husband for his daughter.

有 一首老鼠娶新娘的童謠：

一月一，年初一。一月二，年初二。

年初三，早上床，今夜老鼠娶新娘。

在台灣的習俗中，年初三是老鼠娶新娘的日子，你知道它的由來嗎？

傳說從前在一個農莊的牆腳下，有個老鼠村。

村長的女兒很漂亮，村裡的小夥子都想娶她做新娘。村長不曉得該把女兒嫁給誰才行。

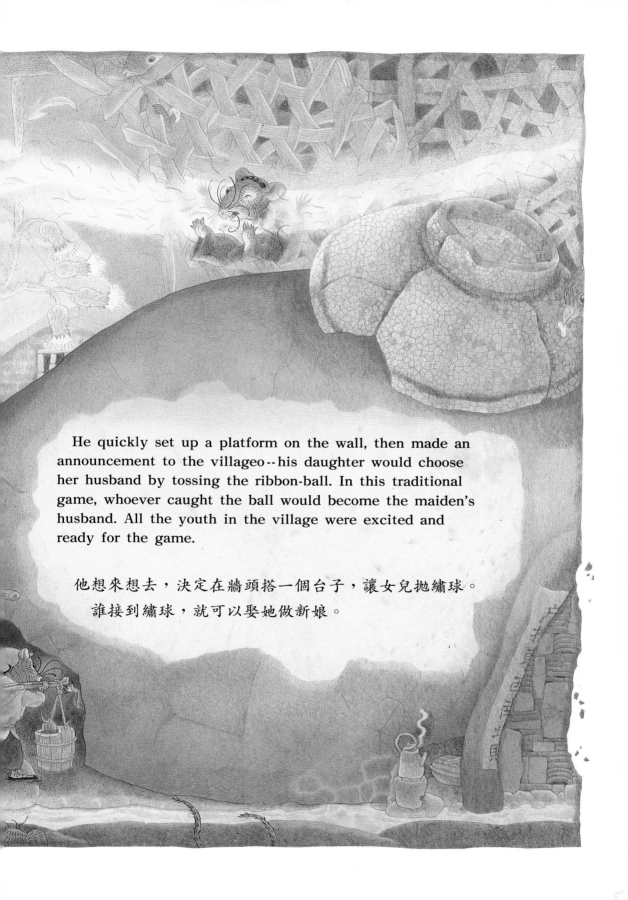

He quickly set up a platform on the wall, then made an announcement to the villageo--his daughter would choose her husband by tossing the ribbon-ball. In this traditional game, whoever caught the ball would become the maiden's husband. All the youth in the village were excited and ready for the game.

他想來想去，決定在牆頭搭一個台子，讓女兒拋繡球。
誰接到繡球，就可以娶她做新娘。

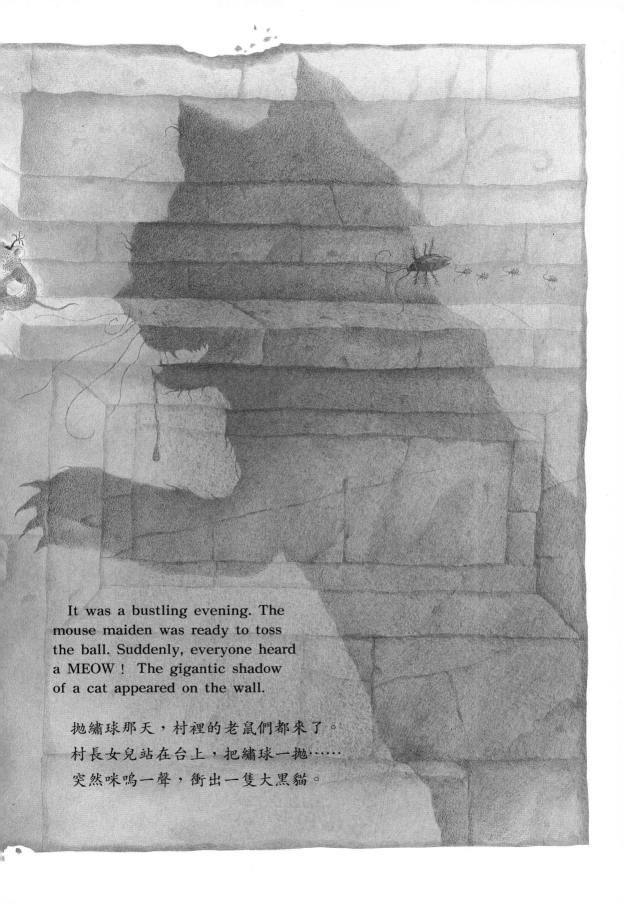

It was a bustling evening. The
mouse maiden was ready to toss
the ball. Suddenly, everyone heard
a MEOW! The gigantic shadow
of a cat appeared on the wall.

拋繡球那天，村裡的老鼠們都來了。
村長女兒站在台上，把繡球一拋……
突然咪嗚一聲，衝出一隻大黑貓。

A Cat ! The big black cat lunged at the ribbon-ball. Its claws swiped at the platform, smashing everything to pieces. Every mouse fled, screaming. The mouse maiden was so scared that she fell from the wall. She was caught by a young mouse named Ah-Lang, who grabbed her hand and ran away.

老鼠們嚇得吱吱亂叫，不知道該往哪裡逃。大黑貓一爪打倒高台，村長女兒從半空中掉下來。幸好一個叫阿郎的小夥子接住她，拉著她的手就跑。

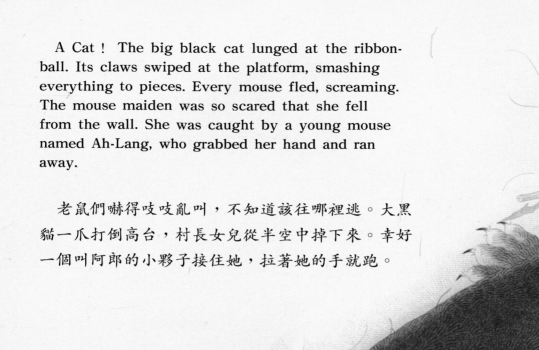

In his dreams that night, the head mouse saw the big black cat catch his daughter. He heard her screams and wails. Then he woke up, and found himself trembling all over.

Holding a pillow to himself, he began to think. What could he do to protect her? Finally, he sat up in bed and decided what to do. He would find the strongest husband in the world for her. Much stronger than the cat.

晚上，村長做了一個惡夢。他夢見大黑貓打爛村子，村長女兒被黑貓抓住，嚇得吱吱叫。

村長嚇醒了，鑽進被窩一邊發著抖一邊說：「太可怕了。為了女兒的幸福，我一定要為她找一個比貓還強，全世界最強的女婿！」

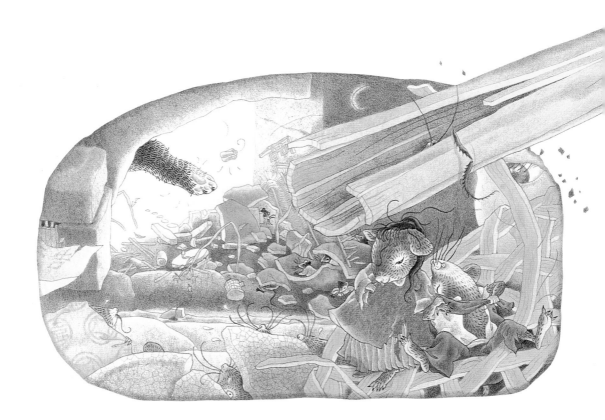

But who could be the strongest in the whole world? He thought and thought until dawn broke. The sun beams gently touched upon his face through the roof cracks. The head mouse was instantly on his feet yelling, "The Sun! The Sun is the strongest in the world. For no one can live, nor can anything grow if the Sun does not shine. I shall marry my daughter to the Sun."

He immediately packed his knapsack and went off to find the Sun.

誰比貓還強？誰是全世界最強的？村長想來想去，好煩惱。

這時天漸漸亮了。陽光從破屋頂照進來，射在村長臉上。

老鼠村長跳起來大叫：「我知道了！太陽是全世界最強的。沒有太陽，就沒有光明；萬物也不能生長。對！我要把女兒嫁給太陽。」

村長說完，急急忙忙出門去找太陽。

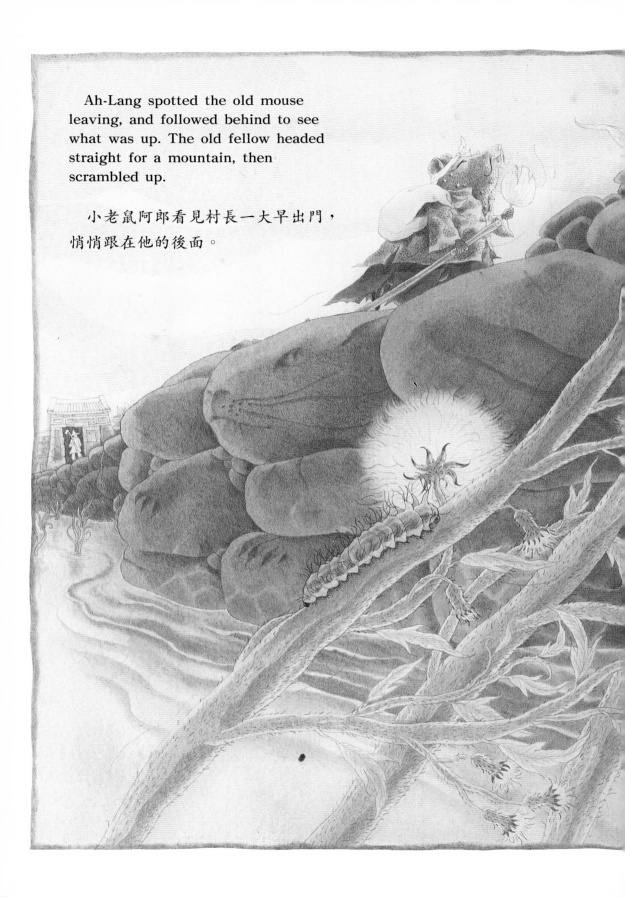

Ah-Lang spotted the old mouse
leaving, and followed behind to see
what was up. The old fellow headed
straight for a mountain, then
scrambled up.

小老鼠阿郎看見村長一大早出門，
悄悄跟在他的後面。

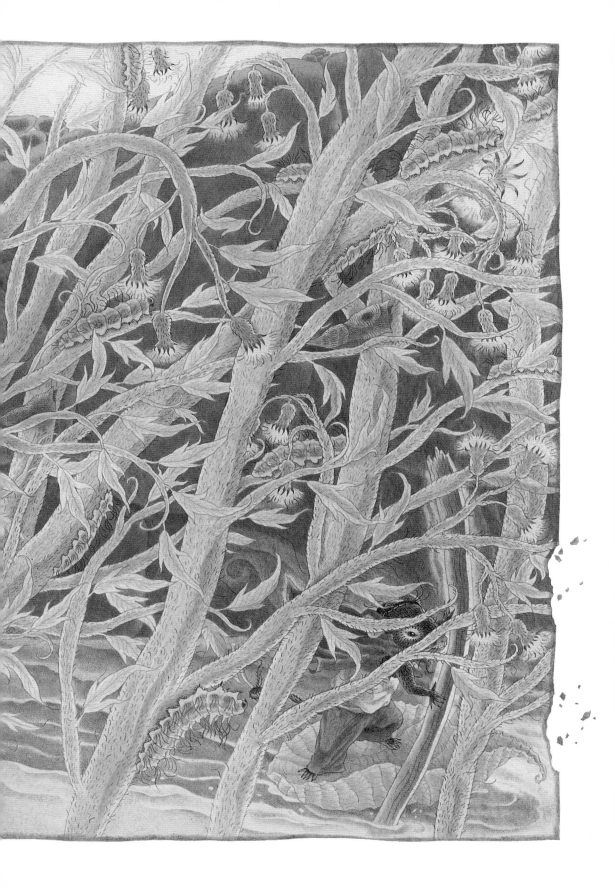

Standing on the mountain top, the mouse leader said to the Sun, "Excuse me, are you the strongest in the world?" Bursting with light and heat, the Sun answered, "Of course, I am ! No one can resist my great power."

The old mouse announced, "I am the mouse leader, and I want to marry my daughter to you." But before he could finish his sentence, a dark Cloud emerged and covered the Sun.

　　村長走好久，終於爬上山頂。他問太陽:「你是全世界最強的嗎?」

　　太陽得意的放出全身的光和熱，説:「當然，我是全世界最強的。世界上有誰能抵擋我的光和熱?」

　　村長擦著頭上的汗説:「我是老鼠村的村長，我要把女兒嫁給你。」

　　村長的話還沒説完，忽然一片烏雲飄來，遮住了太陽。

The old mouse was stunned. But he quickly got his wits back and proposed to the Cloud, with both arms wide, "Excuse me, I am the mouse leader and I want to marry my daughter to you. Are you the strongest in the world?"

The Cloud proudly grinned, "Of course I am! I am the only one that can block the Sun's light and heat." But before the Cloud could finish his sentence, a fierce Wind arose and blew the Cloud away.

村長看見烏雲遮住太陽，連忙大聲說：「我是老鼠村的村長，我要把女兒嫁給全世界最強的。你是不是全世界第一強？」

烏雲笑著說：「沒錯，我就是全世界第一強，因為只有我才能遮住炎熱的陽光。」

烏雲的話還沒說完，一陣風吹過來，把烏雲吹散了。

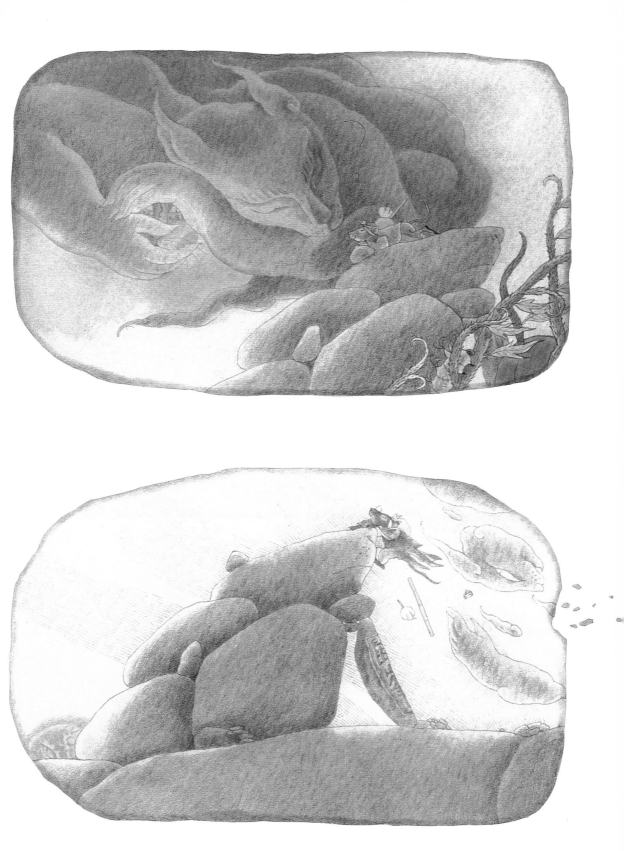

The leader turned to the Wind and said again, "Excuse me, I am the mouse leader and I want to marry my daughter to you. Are you the strongest in the world?"

"Of course I am！ I can blow away the Cloud, I can blow the hat off your head, and I can even blow you back to your house." The Wind blew up a gale that threw the old mouse high into the sky. He flew along swiftly until‑‑Bang！‑‑he crashed into the village wall and dropped to the ground. Meanwhile, Ah-Lang was blown into the river and struggled to swim to shore.

老鼠村長對風說:「我在找全世界最強的,好把女兒嫁給他。你知不知道,世界上誰最強?」

風說:「全世界誰能比我強?我會吹,吹散烏雲,吹掉人們的帽子,也能把你吹回家。」

風鼓起嘴「呼」的吹出一陣強風,把村長吹得半天高。

吹得正高興,碰到一堵牆。老鼠村長重重的撞在牆上,撞得眼發花。

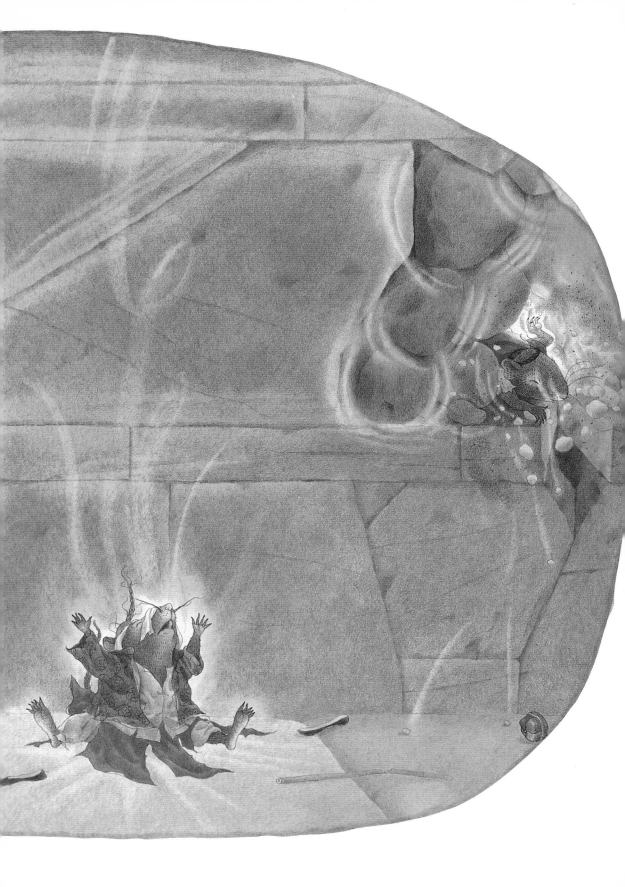

The old mouse rubbed his behind. He looked up at the Wall, then again said, "Excuse me, I am the mouse leader and I want to marry my daughter to you. Are you the strongest in the world?"

The Wall answered, "Of course I am! I fear nothing on heaven or earth. The strongest··· OOUUCCH! Forgot to tell you," the Wall complained, "the one thing I fear is the Mouse." A brick fell, and out came Ah-Lang. He bowed and handed the old mouse his hat.

The old mouse finally realized that mice may be small, but they have skills that no others have. So he said to Ah-Lang, "You are the strongest of all. I will marry my daughter to you."

老鼠村長跌在地上，一邊揉著屁股，對牆說：「牆啊牆，你是不是全世界最強？我想把女兒嫁給你做新娘。」

牆挺著胸回答：「我天不怕地不怕，我是天下第一強！」牆正說著，忽然大叫一聲「哎喲!」只見牆腳破了一個洞，洞中鑽出小阿郎。

牆小聲的說：「我天不怕地不怕，就怕老鼠來打洞。」

老鼠村長這才知道，原來老鼠雖小，也有別人比不上的本事呢。他高興的對阿郎說：「我決定把女兒嫁給你。」

The mouse leader then prepared the traditional wedding for his daughter. On her wedding day, the beautiful bride sat on a wicker-shoe sedan chair, carried by two mice. Her dowry was put into many, many cases and carried by other mice.

就在三月初三，村長女兒坐著草鞋做的花轎，
吹吹打打嫁給阿郎。

When the bride and bridegroom arrived at his parents' house, they knelt down and bowed to them. Once, twice, three times. All the villagers watched, then joined the happy wedding party.

　　從此，年初三老鼠娶新娘的傳說，便流傳下來。每到這天，孩子總愛唱著：小白菜，地裡黃，老鼠村，老村長，村長女兒美叮噹，想找女婿比貓強。太陽最強嫁太陽，太陽不行嫁給雲，雲不行，嫁給風，風不行，嫁給牆，牆不行，想一想，還是嫁給老鼠郎。花對花，柳對柳，雞嫁雞，狗嫁狗。畚箕畚箕配掃帚。

　　一月一，年初一。一月二，年初二。年初三，早上床，今夜老鼠娶新娘。大小老鼠來幫忙，抬花轎，搬嫁妝，新郎新娘早拜堂。一拜堂，二拜堂，三拜堂來入洞房。

繪本童話中國

老鼠娶新娘

文／張玲玲　　圖／劉宗慧

發行人／王榮文　　出版發行／遠流出版事業股份有限公司

地址／台北市汀州路 3 段 184 號 7 樓之 5　　郵撥／0189456-1

電話／886-2-23651212　　傳眞／886-2-23657979

1992 年 10 月 20 日初版 1 刷

2000 年 3 月 15 日初版 11 刷

行政院新聞局局版臺業字第 1295 號

著作權顧問／蕭雄淋律師

法律顧問／王秀哲律師・董安丹律師

ISBN／957-32-2703-7

定價120元

The Mouse Bride

Retold by Monica Chang; Illustrated by Lesley Liu.

Copyright ⓒ 1995 by Yuan-Liou Publishing Co., Ltd.

7F-5, 184, Sec. 3 Ding Chou Rd., Taipei, Taiwan, R.O.C.

TEL: (886-2)3651212　FAX: (886-2)3657979

Printed in Taiwan

Summary:

A mouse goes to the sun, cloud, wind,

and wall in search of the strongest husband for his daughter,

only to find him among his own kind.